We Share EVERYTHING!

by Robert Munsch

illustrated by
Michael Martchenko

SCHOLASTIC CANADA LTD.
New York Toronto London Auckland Sydney
Mexico City New Delhi Hong Kong Buenos Aires

*The illustrations in this book were painted in watercolour
on Crescent illustration board.*

This book was designed in QuarkXPress, with type set in 18 point Caslon 244.

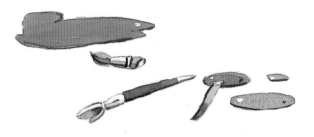

www.scholastic.ca

Canadian Cataloguing in Publication Data
Munsch, Robert N., 1945 –
We share everything!

ISBN 0-590-51450-4

I. Martchenko, Michael. II. Title.

PS8576.U575W4 1999a   jC813'.54   C98-930258-2
PZ M85We 1999a

ISBN-10 0-590-51450-4 / ISBN-13 978-0-590-51450-7

40 39 38 37 36   Printed in Malaysia   108   16 17 18 19 20

*O*n their very first day of school,

when they didn't know what to do,

Amanda and Jeremiah walked into the kindergarten classroom and Amanda picked up a book.

Jeremiah came over to her and said, "Give me that book."

Amanda said, "No, I won't give you this book. I'm looking at this book."

So Jeremiah tried what worked with his little brother. He said, "If you don't give me that book, I am going to yell and scream."

"Too bad!" said Amanda.

So Jeremiah opened his mouth really wide and screamed:

"AAAAAAAAHHHHH!"

Amanda stuck the book in his mouth:

BLUMPH!

Jeremiah said, "GAWCK!"

The teacher came running over
and said,
    "Now, LOOK!
This is kindergarten.
In kindergarten we share.
We share *everything*."
    "Okay, okay, okay, okay, okay,"
said Amanda and Jeremiah.

Jeremiah started to build a tower with blocks.

Amanda came over and said, "Give me those blocks."

"I won't give you the blocks," said Jeremiah. "I'm building a tower."

So Amanda tried what worked with her older brother. She said, "If you don't give me those blocks, I am going to kick them down!"

"Too bad," said Jeremiah.

So Amanda kicked the blocks:

CRASH!

Blocks went all over the floor.
Amanda yelled:

Ouch!

Owww!

Ouch!

Owww!

Ouch!

Ouch!

Owww!

The teacher came running over
and said,
"Now, LOOK!
This is kindergarten.
In kindergarten we share.
We share *everything*."
"Okay, okay, okay, okay, okay,"
said Amanda and Jeremiah.

Then Jeremiah and Amanda
went to play with the paint.

"I'm first," said Jeremiah.

"No! I'm first," said Amanda.

"If you don't let me go first,"
said Jeremiah, "I am going to yell
and scream."

"Too bad," said Amanda.

So Jeremiah and Amanda were both first,
and paint went flying all over the room.

Jeremiah yelled as loud as he could:

"AAAAAAHHHHHH!"

The teacher and all the kids
came running over and said,
"Now, LOOK!
This is kindergarten.
In kindergarten we share.
We share *everything*."

So Jeremiah looked at Amanda and said, "Okay, Amanda, we are supposed to share. What are we going to share?"

"I don't know," said Amanda. "Let's share . . . let's share . . . let's share our shoes."

"Good idea!" said Jeremiah.

So they shared their shoes and Jeremiah said, "Look at this. Pink shoes, and they fit just right. My mom never gets me pink shoes. This is great! Let's share . . . Let's share . . . Let's share our shirts."

So they shared their shirts, and Jeremiah said, "Look at this. A pink shirt. No other boy in kindergarten has a pink shirt."

"Yes," said Amanda. "This is fun. Let's share . . . Let's share . . . Let's share our pants."

So they shared their pants.

"Wow!" said Jeremiah. "Pink pants!"

The teacher came back and said, "Oh, Jeremiah and Amanda. You're sharing, and you're learning how to act in kindergarten, and you're being very grown-up, and Jeremiah, I really like your . . . PINK PANTS! Jeremiah, where did you get those pink pants?"

"Oh," said Jeremiah, "It's okay. Amanda and I shared our clothes."

The teacher yelled, "What have you done? Who said you could share your clothes?"

And all the kids said:
"Now, LOOK!
This is kindergarten.
In kindergarten
we share . . . "

"We share EVERYTHING!"